The Fiddle Ribbon

Special thanks to all the wonderful people who helped me with this book:
Raeann Federici, Mac McLanahan, Sarah McLanahan, Anne
Kaufmann, Don Kaufmann, Mary King, Mike Fischman, Marie
Fitzgerald, Dorothy Goeller and Peter Goranson.
—Margo Lemieux

About the ceilidh—A ceilidh is a social gathering with traditional music, dancing, and storytelling. It has its roots in the Irish and Scottish languages and it is pronounced KAY lee.

Published by Silver Press
A Division of Simon & Schuster
299 Jefferson Road, Parsippany, NJ 07054

Designed by BIG BLUE DOT

Manufactured in the United States of America
10 9 8 7 6 5 4 3 2 1

Library of Congress Cataloging-in-Publication Data
Lemieux, Margo.
The fiddle ribbon/by Margo Lemieux; illustrated by Francis Livingston p. cm.
Summary: While spending the summer helping their grandparents on the farm,
Jennie and Jimmy learn about their Scottish heritage through the fiddle and the step-dance.
[1. Grandparent and child—Fiction. 2. Violin—Fiction. 3. Folk dancing—Fiction.]
I. Livingston, Francis, ill, II. Title.
PZ7.L5373377F1   1996   [E]—dc20 95-19536   CIP   AC
ISBN 0-382-39096-2 (LSB)   ISBN 0-382-39097-0 (JHC)   ISBN 0-382-39098-9 (pbk.)

The Fiddle Ribbon

written by Margo Lemieux
illustrated by Francis Livingston

Jennie always hummed. Before she could talk, she hummed little tunes her dad taught her, songs she heard on the radio, nursery rhymes—even some little made-up tunes that were happy and sad at the same time.

She sat at breakfast, hugging her knees, humming an angry song. How did Mom and Dad expect their kids to give up the whole summer to go north and help grandparents they hardly even knew?

"Grandma doesn't get around so well and Papa is, well, just getting old," Dad said. "They could use some extra hands."

Jimmy danced around the kitchen. "I'll miss the soccer playoffs," he groaned.

Mom sighed. "One child who can't sit still and one child who can't be quiet. What am I to do?"

On the plane Jennie hummed the whole time, driving
Jimmy crazy. Jimmy drove the other passengers crazy by
fidgeting in his seat and shuffling his feet.

Papa and Grandma's white farmhouse sat on a knoll at the
very edge of the rocky, windswept coast. The air was sweet
and fresh, and wildflowers framed the fields.

Papa and Grandma were cheerful, but it was not much fun for a girl who was used to having her friends around and a gym and pool within walking distance. Lucky Jimmy made friends with Patrick on the next farm and usually disappeared after supper to visit.

Sometimes she hummed to herself, sad little tunes that blew away in the wind.

One day Jennie and Papa were picking tiny wild blueberries.

Papa was humming.

"That's a pretty song," she said.

"It's a fiddle tune that my grandmother brought from her homeland," he said. "It's for dancing." He hummed louder and faster. "When we go back to the house, I'll show you the fiddle."

Picking blueberries was hot work in spite of the wind so they drank lemonade in the shade on the porch.

The worn leather fiddle case was lined with faded red velvet. As Papa picked up the fiddle, the sun turned the polished wood golden.

Papa settled the curved instrument under his chin and played a quick little tune that was happy and sad at the same time, much like Jennie's humming songs. "Hold it just so and draw it lightly, like this."

She tucked the fiddle under her chin and grasped the bow. Slowly she drew the bow across the strings. The beautiful, graceful violin let out a rusty screech like an angry crow.

She and Papa laughed.

"That's how I sounded at first," he said. "My grandmother taught me to play when I was even younger than you."

Jennie tried again, but the noise was even worse.

"Is that a moose on my porch?" Grandma said, and they all laughed.

"Your grandfather can make that fiddle sing like a thrush," she said. "The first time I heard him at the ceilidh, I knew he was the man for me."

Papa smiled. "Not everyone liked my fiddling, eh,"
he said. "Life on a farm is hard work, and when I'd sneak
off behind the barn to play, my father would bellow,
'Ernest! Get to work and stop foolin' around.'"
"But the music was in his heart," said Grandma.

"That's right. My grandmother who taught me said music is the ribbon that ties people together. It goes on and on from generation to generation and never ends. When she gave me my first fiddle, it was tied with an endless ribbon that she said went on and on like the music. Here, I still have it." He rummaged in the case, moving aside a clean white cloth and a cake of rosin. He held up a dark, scraggly ribbon.

The ribbon was woven together so that it was one big circle.

"See, a ribbon with no end," he said, sliding his fingers along, around and around. As he gazed at it, his eyes were sad. Then he smiled. "Here, little Jennie, let me show you how to draw the bow."

Jennie tried. At first the sound was bitter, but she practiced with determination.

When Jimmy came in, tired from raking hay, he complained, "Is that what you've been doing all afternoon? We're supposed to be helping out, not playing around. I could hear that racket way out in the field."

Jennie did feel bad because she was supposed to be
helping. From then on she only played after she had
finished her chores—behind the barn where Jimmy
couldn't hear or after supper when he was visiting Patrick.
Pretty soon she could pick out some of the little tunes she
had in her head and some of the ones Papa showed her.

One night Jimmy said, "Patrick says there's going to be a ceilidh next week. Can I go?"

"Why, I thought we'd all go," said Grandma. "Your mother and father will be here."

Jimmy grinned. "Do you think Mom and Dad will like it?"

Jennie thought of her parents in their business clothes. She couldn't picture them enjoying themselves in a barn.

"Well," said Papa, "your father used to like it."

Mom and Dad arrived the night of the ceilidh, tired and out of sorts from the long drive. They sat down to the delicious meat pie and fresh vegetables Jennie and Grandma had prepared.

"I'm learning to play the fiddle," said Jennie.

"And I . . .," began Jimmy.

You were supposed to be here helping out," said Dad.

"They were," said Papa firmly. "They were much more than a help."

"Good," said Dad helping himself to another ear of corn. "I had forgotten how good fresh-picked corn is."

"I'll show you all the hay that Jimmy baled and all the blueberries that Jennie put up," said Papa.

"Okay," said Dad, helping himself to another serving of blueberry slump. "I had forgotten how good wild blueberries are," he said, smacking his purple lips.

Mom had a second helping, too.

Everyone in the village came to the barn. Jimmy intro-
duced Patrick, and it turned out Dad had known Patrick's
dad when they were boys.

People played music on fiddles, pipes, accordions, and
guitars. Dancers' feet pounded the floor.

"See how his feet stay close to the floor," said Jimmy
when Patrick got up to dance. "That's called step dancing."

Everyone clapped when Papa took out his fiddle.
Jennie clapped the hardest.
Papa sat on a hard wooden chair in the center of the
room, tucked the fiddle under his chin, and raised the neck
up high. The barn was silent. He began to stamp his feet,
his leather soles clacking on the wooden floor. He lifted the
bow smoothly and the fiddle began to sing.
Everyone cheered.

The music was wild and fast, and Papa's feet danced along to it. People were clapping and stomping. It was hard to sit still.

Each time a dancer got up, Papa played faster, his fingers skimming the strings, the bow pumping up and down, his feet dancing along with them.

Everyone clapped for a long time when Papa finished.
He held up his hands and said, "I have a surprise. My
granddaughter Jennie will now play." He stood and held
out the fiddle to her.

Jennie was frozen. She had thought maybe to play
sometime, but not yet—not tonight!

The fiddle was still warm from Papa's hands, like when she practiced in the sun behind the barn.

She drew the bow.

There was a squawk, like the very first sound she had made on the fiddle but not quite as bad. She stopped. No one laughed and Papa was still smiling.

Then she was all by herself behind the barn again and the music began to come. She couldn't play as fast as Papa but the melody was there, happy and sad at the same time.

Somebody was dancing.

It was Jimmy. His face was solemn but his feet were flinging in time to the music.

Jennie was so startled that she nearly dropped the fiddle. So that was what he had been doing all those evenings at Patrick's.

Instead of stopping, she played faster and he kept right up. Mom and Dad's mouths were wide open.

Jennie's arms were getting tired. How had Papa been able to play so fast for so long? She was just about to finish playing when she saw the people parting to let up another dancer.

It was Grandma.

She briskly moved her cane to the middle of the floor and holding on, she began to do the steps. Her feet still remembered the steps and she put her whole heart into it.

She and Jennie finished at the same time. She held out her arms and Jennie went to hug her.

When people finally stopped cheering, Mom said, "I guess this is what happens when I get one kid who won't sit still and one who can't be quiet—a dancer and a fiddler."

"We'll teach you how to dance, Mom," said Jimmy.

By late August, the winds from the Gulf of Saint Lawrence had a fine nip to them. The family wore sweaters as they gathered on the front porch to say goodbye.

"You kids were a real help," said Papa. "Will you come back next summer?"

"Can we?" Jimmy jumped up and down.

"For you, Jimmy," said Grandma, presenting a box to him.

"All right," said Jimmy, taking cowboy boots from the box.

"And for you, Jennie." Papa gave her a special smile and a package.

"Open it," said Jimmy.

She opened the package. Inside was a brand new fiddle, just like Papa's and wrapped around the fiddle case was a bright fresh ribbon woven in a circle so that it had no end.

The following is a fiddle tune that Jennie might have learned to play.

THE NURSERYMAN

Miss McPherson Grant's
Jig of Ballindalloch

William Marshall